Less Boring

Book 1

Rohan Gedall

Copyright © Rohan Gedall

Published by

From Words to Worlds,

Lausanne, Switzerland

www.fromwordstoworlds.com

Cover by Gary Edward Gedall

Print Edition
ISBN: **2-940535-44-6**
ISBN 13: **978-2-940535-44-6**

About the Author

Rohan Gedall

Rohan is Swiss, with an English father and a Romanian mother.

He speaks 3 languages, (French, English and Romanian).

He plays both flute and piano to a quite high level.

He also rides, (American style) and enjoys playing tennis and table tennis.

And the 'Scribe'

Gary Edward Gedall.

Gary is a practicing psychologist, state registered psychotherapist.

He also writes as a hobby and has self-published 11 books; inspirational novels, books on psychology, hypnosis, and self-help.

Disclaimer:

The characters and events related in our books are a synthesis of all that we have seen and done, the people that we have met and their stories.

Hence, there are events and people that have echoes with real people and real events, however no character is taken purely from any one person and is in no way intended to depict any person, living or dead.

Table of Contents

Less Boring

Preface

"You'll see, it'll be … better." The piercing, green eyes of the witch, crinkled in an all too infrequent smile. The little hunched person looked up from serving breakfast.

"Yes, of course, you're totally right." Clearly not having the slightest idea of what she was referring to.

"Those humans have become so boring." Carefully sliding her long, black nails between the handle and the teacup.

"Since they all declared peace and became reasonable. They do nothing but go to work, do their sport and sleep.

Oh God, give me a break!"

"Yes, Ma'am, a break, you're totally right."

"What fun is it watching them, if they never do anything stupid anymore?"

"Yes, Ma'am, nothing stupid," as he serves her a healthy portion of stewed spiders, in her favourite skull bowl.

Patricia swanned down the Champs Elysées, her beautiful golden hair tossed by the gentle breeze.

Her gold tipped, leopard skin boa, trailing along the famous pavement.

She looked at her gold and diamond studded watch as it began to beep…

"Merde, shit, it's already after seven."

Patricia drags herself out of her, miserable, single bed, into the antique bathroom, the plumbing is definitely historic.

She turns on the tap of the chipped wash basin, and waits for a long moment.

And finally, after giving up on any chance of hot water, splashes several handfuls of lukewarm liquid on her face, and returns to her untidy bedroom.

" 'kay, I'm washed, time to get dressed."

Hygiene is not her highest priority, that being MONEY…

Once out of the metro, she grabs herself a croissant and a café au lait, and hurries into work.

She is employed in one of the most modern, high rise buildings in Paris.

Unfortunately, carrying out one of the most boring jobs in that building.

She is the assistant, of the assistant, to one of the sociological researchers working there.

Her job is to enter the statistical information that has been gathered by the investigating teams.

"So important. I must be saving the world.

Somehow, I'm protecting against the next major plague. So important, to know just exactly how many times Parisians brush their teeth every day."

Her boss strolls into her cubical and absently picks up the pile of papers waiting to be entered onto the system.

As if she can judge, just by their weight, how much Patricia is behind with her work.

"I've known faster typists than you. Sometimes, I even think that a statue might type faster than you do."

'If she was a statue, at least she would shut up,' Patricia mumbles to herself, through clenched teeth.

"What did you say?"

"I said, 'I wish that you would turn into a statue'. A golden statue, then you would at last be worth something."

The now very angry superior stops for the merest second before beginning to reply, and Patricia waits, and waits …

Hans switches the alarm off, just before it rings.

There are the cows to meet, greet, and milk, then he can take the time to shower and shave.

He breakfasts with his old, but dynamic parents, on bread, butter, local cheese and hot, full milk.

As he is about to leave to take the train for work, his mother rushes to hand him his lunch box, full of healthy, local produce. Not forgetting a small bar of famous Swiss chocolate.

At 7.30 am, he is already at his desk preparing his day's work, even though the office doesn't officially open before 8.00.

He likes to arrive early, as it gives him plenty of time to organise himself.

Slowly the office begins to fill up, as his work colleagues arrive, excited to share their experiences over the weekend.

"Awesome party, Saturday."

"Couldn't stay to the end, kids, you know."

"That's what happens when you get old."

Saturday was the birthday of one of the office junior's and she had invited everyone to a BBQ and disco, and it seems that the whole of the team had participated.

"We should do this again soon. Who's up for next weekend?"

"Oh no, I was wrecked all Sunday."

"Yeh, that's the fun."

"Sorry, I've got plans this weekend, what about in two weeks?"

There is a chorus of 'Yes's and 'Great's '.

Then one of the colleagues turns to Hans.

"Didn't notice you on Saturday, didn't you come?"

"Sorry, Karl, but I had other things that had to be done."

"You never seem to have time to do fun things."

"Yes, because life isn't about doing things that you enjoy, life is about enjoying the things that you have to do."

He then turns his attention to the big clock that dominates the room, it is just about to turn eight.

Karl follows Hans's gaze. "How do you do that? You always seem to know exactly when we start, when it's break time, and when to leave?"

"Don't know," Hans shrugs his shoulders, "just instinct, I guess. I've always had a strong connection with time."

"If you have such a good connection with time, why is it that you never have enough time to do fun things?"

"You're repeating yourself," and Hans turns back to his desk and starts his work.

Only, somewhere in the back of his highly organised mind, something has started to tick.

Sometime later, Hans is responding to an email from his boss, asking him for a progress report on his current project.

As there have been some unforeseen production problems that have appeared, he is obliged to explain and to inform his superior, that he will need more time.

More time to complete the job than expected.

" ….. we have unfortunately noticed that the alloy does not yet respond to the specifications, so I need more time …".

Then something very strange happens, and Hans seems to fall into some sort of trance.

He wakes up some moments later, only to discover that he has continued typing without realising."

"I need more time, I need more time, I need more time, I need more time, I need more time, I need more time, I need more time, I need more time, I need more time, I need more time, I need more time, …"

Over and over again, filling his whole computer screen with the phrase.

Hans, shakes himself awake, corrects and completes the email, shuts down his computer and stares in an empty way, vacantly watching the second finger on the authoritative clock, counting down the moments until the end of his shift.

"I need more time," he repeats to himself. "I wish I had more time."

Just then, Karl walks past after going to the vending machine to get himself a coffee. He suddenly notices the Hans is not working but looking towards the clock.

Following Hans's gaze, Karl looks towards
the clock, and not watching where he is
walking, bumps heavily into Hans's desk.

In a flash, Hans realises that if the coffee
splashes onto his computer, it could damage
it and create hours of work to put things right.

"I … need … more … TIME!!" He screams
out, almost in anguish.

The coffee cup drops from Karl's grasp and
plunges towards Hans's desk, very, very
slowly …

"You see, you see, it's already… better."

The piercing, green eyes of the witch, crinkles up in an all too infrequent smile.

The little hunched person looks up from serving lunch.

"Yes, of course, you're totally right." Clearly not having the slightest idea of what she is referring to.

She turns back to him, the magic mirror still reflecting the image of the golden statue.

"It's happening, it's happening," her crazy, toothless grin, cracking up her long, grey face.

"Those humans will now become much less boring." Carefully lacing her long, black nailed fingers around the intricately, decorated, silver fork.

She digs the nasty prongs into the baked, hornet's nest.

She smiles again, noting that it has been cooked to perfection; the hornets, doped by the heat, but still alive, still softly buzzing in their old home.

"How much I love the sound of dying creatures, when I eat."

"Yes, Ma'am, you're totally right."

"It's fun isn't it, watching them, now they're doing stupid things again"

"Yes, Ma'am, stupid, stupid hornets" as he serves her a steaming brew of nettle tea, in her favourite skull bowl.

"Stupid hornets?"

…, and Patricia waits, and waits …

But the reply would never come.

Patricia backs onto the edge of her desk, shocked.

Her angry boss now silently, glittering before her.

Just then, Mathis enters.

She turns to her other superior.

"Patricia, where are you up to entering my latest da… What the ..?"

But the confused, young woman has no reasonable explanation to give him.

"It…, just…, well…, happened," and suddenly she bursts into tears.

The bemused, researcher watches, totally lost, as the sobbing, secretary rushes out of the office.

Caleb Walker is returning from the
Worthington Glacier in Thompson Pass, only
29 miles from Valdez's city centre.

He has just left the small group of tourists at
the Keystone hotel, euphoric but exhausted
after their tour of the glacier.

However, Caleb has seen this scenery all of
his life, it holds no thrill for him.

He heads into a small, a near-by pub and orders himself a glass of Vodka and a half of indigenous beer.

As it is quite early, there are only a few local alcoholics hanging around, starting to drink before the crowds arrive.

However, the term, crowd, does not have exactly the same meaning here than in other more populated regions of the earth.

Their continual animated conversations create a backdrop of loud buzzing, like a small swarm of excited hornets.

Josh, the short, hairy barman brings Caleb his drinks. And having absolutely nothing better to do, hangs around for a chat.

"How's your day?"

"Same as always, white."

"White?"

"Sure, the snow tends to be coloured like that." Caleb lifts the small glass and empties it in one swallow. The barman smiles.

"Well, you could be right there, snow does tend to be rather white looking."

Caleb's still purple lips, dip into a reflective frown. "Don't you think that that is boring?"

"But what do you expect? Snow is white. Another?" He offers to refill his beaker.

The tall, heavy guide, proffers his empty glass, and waits, thoughtfully while it is replenished.

"And how would it be if snow could be different colours?"

"Is this all that you've drunk today?" Caleb notices Josh's concerned tone of voice.

He takes a moment to take another sip of his beer.

Calmly and quietly he stops for a moment and then smiles.

He gently returns the glass to the polished, counter top…

"Isn't it normal to have dreams?"

Wiping dry a glass, he responds with a rather forced smile. "Sure."

Tears well up in his eyes as he swallows down his vodka. "My dream is to be able to change the colour of stuff."

"What, like this vodka?" He laughs, as he moves to refill the glass of another drinker, sitting alone at the other end of the bar.

Caleb, smiles to himself as he fantasises his response to the question.

"What the Hell have you given me?!"

He is shocked out of his reverie by the man's
exclamation. Intrigued, he walks down to see
what the problem is.

Only to discover the stunned client, gazing,
confused at the bright, pink liquid, just
poured into his shot glass.

There he stands, immobilised, unable to
believe his eyes.

Minutes pass, but he fails to register any more
of the conversation.

Then, he blinks twice, shakes his head in
disbelief, and still troubled, leaves.

Patricia is sitting with her knees pulled up towards her chest, rocking slightly from side to side, and quietly mumbling to herself.

'No, no it can't be, it can't be me, no, no it's not.' And having come to the end of that long reflection, gets up and makes herself a cup of instant coffee.

She takes the steaming liquid and takes a small sip, and frowns.

"Alcohol would be better."

Not many moments later, she slips on her blue, worn military jacket and goes hunting for a cheap bottle of red wine.

The street is still quite full of people, as it is only early evening.

The local supermarket is only a few blocks down, and before she realises it, she is already scanning the shelves for something inexpensive but not too disgusting.

Being Paris, there happens to be quite a wide selection to choose from.

Eventually she makes her choice and goes to wait at the single, staffed checkout.

The queue edges forward, and finally she gets to the front when a little old lady arrives with just a packet of sugar.

"Would it be okay if I just passed in front of you? My husband is waiting to get his milky tea, and I have forgotten to buy any sugar."

Patricia feels the eyes of all the other customers and the cashier willing her to let the woman pass.

She frowns, beaten by the expectations of the crowd of nice people, mumbles something and steps to one side.

The pensioner hurries to the counter and shows the package to the man who rings up the sale.

A spotted, shaking hand, slips into the heavy coat and draws out a handful of small change…

With nightmare slowness, she starts to examine each coin, painfully reflecting on its current value. The desk Buddha smiles benignly as the money piles up by tiny increments.

Long minutes pass, fading in and out of this reality.

"Next."

She is awoken out of her dream-state and finally takes her place at the counter.

Smilingly, the cashier, takes the bottle and scans the striped bar-code.

Sighing, Patricia slides her smooth, steady hand into her worn, jacket pocket, to pull out her fake, leopard skin purse.

Only, it is sitting, sedately waiting for her on her untidy hall table.

"Merde". All that she can find is a handful of small coins that must have dropped into her pocket, as if by accident.

And so, here she stands, vaguely looking at the loose change, not capable to continue with any appropriate gesture.

He looks up at her from behind his cash register, expectant.

"Unless those are silver coins, I'm afraid that I don't believe that they will be enough."

"Actually, gold would be even better." And, still as if half in a dream, she demands for the coins to turn into the precious, yellow metal.

And then, frustrated, throws them in the counter top, and, almost crying, leaves the establishment.

Suddenly she feels a hand grabbing her by the shoulder.

"What the …?" She turns sharply round, ready to hit out at her assailant.

"Don't hit me, don't hit me," the shop assistant cowers down in fear.

"What?" She is icily cold and aggressive.

"Look," he holds out his hand and opens it to her amazement. He is clutching a fistful of shiny, metal coins…

Gold.

The children are still filing back into class after the lunchbreak.

Miss Thatcher stands impatiently in front of the impeccably clean blackboard.

Late again, the children have absolutely no respect for time.

"Respect," as she had just been reflecting, as usual, to the ever-patient principle, "they are severely lacking in any idea of what that means.

Of course, I blame the parents, it is not their fault the little dears, but it needs to be dealt with."

'That John's hair, it is so much too long. Alice Davenport, skirt, still much too short. David Hughes, slouching again.

Alvin Marks, wearing sneakers…'. So many things that are not as they ought to be.

"When you finally manage to get to your seats, please can you open your Debrett's at page 230. Today we will read about Wimbledon."

The children dive into their desks and extract their now worn copies of 'Debrett's New Guide to Etiquette and Modern Manners.'

"David, would you have the kindness to please start reading from the beginning of the section?" She smiles helpfully at the lost looking, ten-year-old.

"And, please, try to sit up a little straighter, and speak clearly and with conviction."

He takes a long moment to find the aforementioned passage, as if by taking all this time, there could be the hope that she might possibly think to change her mind and choose another victim.

"We only have ninety-minute periods, David, so it would help if you would make an effort to be a little more efficacious."

Letting the complexity of her remark pass literally over his head, he finds the correct text and starts to read in a small, hesitant voice.

"Wimbledon. The apex of the tennis year, Wimbledon is the only Grand Slam tournament played on grass."

"I am not deaf, but I cannot understand anything that you are reading, please David, sit up straighter, breath deeper and enunciate clearly."

"It is held at the All England Lawn Tennis and Croquet Club every year in June or July…"

"David, louder" The exasperation clearly expressed in her shrill voice.

"Tickets are highly sought after and need to be …"

"David Hughes, I have asked you to sit up straight and speak loudly and clearly. I wish that you would do as I say!" Her voice is tense, and difficulty controlled.

Suddenly, as if struck by some invisible lightning bolt, he jolts in shock, back, ramrod straight, voice clear and round as a BBC announcer.

" … applied for from the club between August and December of the preceding …"

The administrative staff are still filing back into the open-plan office space after the lunchbreak.

Hans sits perplexed in front of his impeccably tidy desk.

Late again, these people have absolutely no respect for time.

He gets the impression that as they pass by his workspace, they are glancing at him and their conversation suddenly ceases.

This only adds to his feeling of perplexity.

Of course, they would all be talking about what happened. If he had someone to talk with, so would he.

But as he always stays at his desk at lunchtime, to eat his healthy, balanced lunch, there is no opportunity to share with anyone else, the weird event of this morning.

Once, out of earshot, they would restart their discussions. Their continual animated conversations create a backdrop of loud buzzing, like a small swarm of excited hornets.

He finds himself shaking his head, as if to dislodge the sounds, 'no, no, no, no, they have no idea of what they are talking about'.

Hans can guess just how much they must be speculating on what happened, but theirs is likely to only be idle chatter.

They have surely not spent most of this
lunchbreak, surfing the internet, trying to find
any reference to such an occurrence.

Although he has succeeded to find some odd
reports of other, unexplainable events, he has
yet to find anything linked to the extension of
time.

Last to re-enter, pretty much as usual, Karl
swans in to their workplace.

On noticing Hans, he marches directly up to
his desk.

"Hi Flash, had a 'Quickpot', for lunch, did
we?" His attempt at humour, to normalise the
situation, unfortunately seems heavy, and not
really funny.

Hans can easily feel his discomfort but is still
very appreciative that he is at least trying to
find a way to be as normal as possible.

"No, I'm much more into, good old slow-
food," he smiles back at his work ally.

Karl is leaning over the desk, facing the other, his hands flat on the smooth, white surface.

His colleague, advances his hands, vibrating with inner tension, to contact and cover those of his interlocutor.

Then slowly raises his head, to look directly into the other's eyes, in an emotionally charged whisper.

"What the fuck is going on?"

"What the fuck is going on?"

The usual icy wind hits him full in the face as he re-enters the already dark street. The soft balls of orange light, do little to illumine the sad walk home.

Caleb is wondering how he could be so intoxicated, having only drunk so little.

He has spoken out loud, not that there are any people close enough to hear him.

It doesn't take long for him to arrive in his small, but cosy, wood-lined apartment.

He opens the door, removes his boots, and then, mechanically, walks over to his bed-settee.

Then, without bothering either to open it out or remove any of his clothing, he just flops, exhausted into the soft, welcoming oblivion of sleep.

The restaurant is particularly full, and they had to wait the longest time to be served. She was having quite some difficulty using a knife and fork.

"That's often a problem when you invite a unicorn for dinner," Obama smiles at him, in a friendly way.

He looks up from his green and yellow striped, grilled rib steak, to acknowledge the ex-president's reflection.

The waiter arrives with the next course.

"I'm sorry, but I prefer my umbrellas to be less green," Elvis, as usual, is being a little difficult to satisfy.

"I'm so sorry, I will order you a new batch." Caleb, waves to the server, "it's fine, the umbrellas will be okay". He glares, menacingly at Elvis.

"And the toilet paper is totally on key. Just because they haven't sung any of your songs, don't make a scene."

Elvis frowns, "you have a very suspicious mind, but they could still have included some real classics in their repertoire."

Einstein turns towards him, "Fuck off you ignoramus, you know nothing about music," and starts a heavy double beat on his worn-out drum kit.

The toilet paper turns to the genius and gives him a high-five. "Good on you, pops."

The music increases and increases in volume until he has no choice but to turn over and switch off his alarm clock.

The bottle is almost empty, and her head is gently spinning to the rhythm of Camille.

She is proclaiming just how much that she really doesn't want to get out of the shower.

Patricia can totally relate to this, as her apartment is particularly underheated.

And sometimes, even getting out of her outside clothes can take a real effort of willpower.

For the thousandth time she picks up and examines the golden, one, two and five cent pieces.

Still totally under the shock of all the day's events, the idea to numb the overwhelming feelings of loss of control, seemed to be the best strategy that she could think of, in the moment.

Unfortunately, it is still not having the desired effect, even after most of the bottle of red.

She shakes her head, 'stop thinking, keep drinking, it'll be better in the morning', at least that's what her Facebook friend Jan, would surely say.

And so she dutifully finishes off the rest of the warming, ruby liquid.

She then passes a long quarter of an hour staring vaguely at the ceiling, before abandoning the idea of sleep.

"Screw it, I'm going to try and sell this shit!"

And so she digs out her warmest coat from under a lost pile of clothes from her old Ikea wardrobe, and sets out to test the reality of her new found powers.

Danny Trump slumps down on the chair in front of his oversized mirror and aggressively rips off his nose.

The soft, red sphere, bounces harmlessly off of the reflective surface.

He closes his eyes as if to block out the memory of his day.

"Oh, how much I hate kids."

He then, instinctively reaches down for his regular evening medication.

The strong, smooth, bourbon is the only protection that works against this intense anger that boils up inside, on a daily basis.

However, even before the soothing beverage has time to begin to work its magic, the door behind opens and closes.

"You'd better put that bottle down and stick your nose back on, your shift isn't over yet."

"But it's already after seven thirty, and I'm done for tonight."

"You were informed that there is a late birthday party, and you have to cover all birthdays, it's in your contract."

Danny would really love to suggest to him, exactly where to shove his contract, but he has bills to pay and cannot afford to lose yet another job.

And so he turns, an enormous smile breaking out on his face, even enhanced by the clown's makeup, that he is wearing.

"Sure, no problem, Steve, I'll be right there."

"Great, and don't forget to spray."

"Be right there," he repeats, turning back towards the mirror to hunt out his rubber nose.

Two or three blasts of double-mint breath freshener and he is now ready to return to the arena and face the horribly irritating, munchkin lions.

"Hi kids, let's have fun," he bursts onto the scene.

Actually, the bourbon is helping, as he senses a certain distance from the awful reality of what he is forcing himself to do.

At last the balloons are all given out, the games are done.

And the children are finally sat down at the tables, to stuff themselves with the most unhealthy food that has ever been invented.

Danny has, at the same time, completely formulated how to reorganise his garage and a long, complicated, amusing speech that he would imagine giving to the state senate.

A wonderful and thoughtful speech, explaining exactly why all children under sixteen years old should be sent to Europe to be educated.

He now plans to fade out of the room and return to his evening ritual of getting totally plastered.

Unfortunately, he has not taken into account the bored parents, that are just looking for anything to do or say to pass the unforgiving minutes.

A usual American custom, when there is nothing else to do or to say, is to cover their discomfort with a thick layer of enthusiastic complements.

"Wow, you're so good with the children."

"Do you have a special training program, that you go through, to be so good?"

"It is so kind and generous of you to stay so late to entertain our kids."

Danny, completely blocked by them, wishes that he was a quarterback with a series of enormous line backers to knock each of them, heavily to the ground.

"I just so love this job. Kids are my passion, I would be happy to stay all night, if I could."

"You are so good with them; do you have any special secrets of how to best educate them?"

"Love 'em, that's really all there is to it. If you give them lots of love, then they will respond." He smiles in the most open and winning fashion.

And, before they have the opportunity to ask even one more stupid, inane, ridiculous question, he is gone and back with his bottle.

The bell rings; usually the class would be ready at the starting blocks, and, once signalled, catapult themselves into the scrummage at the door, to reach the relative peace of the playground.

Only, now, here, today, nobody dares to move.

Miss Thatcher stands immobile in front of the impeccably clean blackboard.

She, to be totally honest is just as mesmerised as the children.

David has read for the full ninety minutes, without stopping. His voice, strong and clear as a church bell, his back, straight as a ruler.

She had let him continue reading, finishing chapter 11, 'In Public', and most of chapter 12, 'Entertaining'.

It is only the recreation bell that has broken the spell.

"Thank you, David, it seems that you have finally succeeded to integrate that which I have been asking of you."

 She then turns smiling to the rest of the class, "you may go now."

Feeling the intense, warm glow of personal satisfaction, she glides towards the staff room, to treat herself to a strong, hot, milky, cup of Tetley's.

Her fine, china cup, (brought from her own house), filled with the steaming, light brown tea, in hand, she has a moment to reflect on the recent events.

'So, I finally managed to get him to sit up and enunciate distinctly. It took some time, but constant and clear directives, are what gets results.'

Satisfied with herself, she picks up a sweet digestive and dunks it elegantly into her beverage.

"Where the fuck do I go now?" The usual icy
wind hits her full in the face as she re-enters
the already dark street.

The soft balls of orange light, do little to
illuminate the sad walk outside of her home.

Patricia is wondering how she could be so
little intoxicated, having drunk so much.

She has spoken out loud, not that there are
any people close enough to hear her.

Although it is not that late, but since the clocks have gone back, night comes early to the capital.

She takes out her smart-phone, sadly shaking her head, only an Iphone 3, feeling, just how miserable it is, having such an old phone.

'Now where can I find someone that might buy these golden cents?' She types in 'buy gold in paris'.

'About 56,700,000 results (0,56 seconds)', her phone flashes back to her. She scans down the list, avidly reading the reviews of the old clients.

After five minutes of information overload, she realises just how cold she is feeling and dives into her local coffee shop to warm up.

"Un café s'il vous plaît. "

The Parisien waiter scowls in acknowledgement of her order.

Patricia totally ignores him, following the usual social habits of the French capital.

He quickly returns and delicately tosses the white cup unto the table.

"Anything else?"

Being so lost in her own thoughts and concerns, she doesn't realise that she is responding out loud.

"Yes, I need to find someone to buy some gold."

Today, is a day of miracles, the waiter smiles.

"I have a cousin that buys and sells gold, he is a good man, you can trust him."

Never, ever, ever trust anyone, that says that you can trust me. Red flag.

"Why should I trust him?"

"Because you know me, and if he crooks you, he'll have to answer to yours truly."

"Oh, thank you," she cannot think of anything more to add, so she just flashes him a nervous smile in appreciation.

The waiter writes the name and address on his order pad, smiles again and walks off.

'Curiouser and curiouser', she feels like Alice in her looking-glass world. She drinks her coffee, and leaves, feeling totally perplexed.

Still partly in another world, she fails to check before stepping off of the pavement, unfortunately in the real world, there are cars.

Suddenly, she hears the blaring of a horn, and the glaring of headlights bearing down on her.

"FUCK!!!"

The world slows as her brain races to find any solution.

The car driver closes his eyes, not wishing to witness the accident which he has failed to avoid.

He feels the thud of the impact, just as the car succeeds to come to a halt.

Not having any other choice, he opens his eyes to see the disaster.

No blood on the windshield.

He slowly opens the door and gets out of the car.

He turns to witness the awful scene that he has imagined.

Only to find, in surprise.

Laying some few metres away.

A shining, yellow mass on the side of the road.

"Where the hell do you think that you're going?"

"Sorry," he must have bumped into the guy, without really noticing.

"Danny, go home."

"Oh, hi, Stevie, goin' home?"

"And so should you."

"What do you care?"

"Sure, I care about all my employees."

"You don't really care about me, do you? You can try telling the truth, for once."

There is something in this specific, direct question and tone of voice that touches the manager in a very particular way.

He suddenly, as if struck by some invisible lightning bolt, jolts in shock, only then to relax, voice soft and mellow as a NBC announcer.

"No," he begins to smile in a very relaxed fashion, "actually you're dead right. I don't give a damn about you. I'd like nothing better than to sack you on the spot."

Danny moves forward to respond, but Steve has not at all finished expressing himself.

"You're a total pain in the arse, if I could get rid of you tonight, you'd have your pay-check in the next five minutes."

"So why don't you then?"

"Unfortunately, the boss's dumb-ass kids sort of like you, and he'd be really pissed if I got rid of you.

And he's also a dumb shit, a total idiot, doesn't know anything about running a franchise.

And as for the customers, well, I think that you know where I'd like to stick them."

Danny reels back in shock and surprise, and they said that he was the one with a drinking problem.

'I don't know what he's had, but it's sure as Hell stronger then my stuff,' he has time to reflect.

"I really think that you should be the one to go home," he smiles, as warmly as possible at his crazy, acting boss.

Once, officially dismissed, he suddenly seems to sober up, blinks in shock and surprise, as if coming out of some type of trance state.

"Yes, yes, I think that I should be off home,
'night," and off he disappears into the gloom.

The usual icy wind hits him full in the face as
Danny turns down another dark street.

The soft balls of yellow light, do little to
illumine the sad walk home.

He is wondering how Steve could be so
intoxicated, having never seen him drinking
anything stronger than soda.

'Home or bar'?

Danny Trump slumps down on the chair in front of his undersized mirror and carefully applies cream to his constantly sore nose.

He closes his eyes as if to block out the image of his day to come.

"Oh, how much I hate kids."

He then, instinctively reaches down for his regular morning medication.

The strong, smooth, bourbon is the only protection that works against this intense anger that boils up inside, on a daily basis.

However, even before the soothing beverage has time to begin to work its magic, the door behind opens and closes.

The only child in the world that he doesn't actively hate enters the room.

"You'd get a move on, or you'll be late again."

"What do you care?"

"Apart from the fact that if you lose another job, you'll be even more behind with your child support payments.

And I'll have to give up my ballet lessons again, I actually care that you have a job for your own good."

He turns and smiles at the budding adolescent.

"Okay, honey, I'm on my way." He gets up to give her a parting, peck on the forehead, but cannot ignore how she pulls back when noticing the strong whiskey on his breath.

"Where is it?"

"Top draw," he admits, as he drags on his old, grey coat and leaves the shabby apartment.

The various noises and strong light of the outdoors, aggresses his oversensitive nerves.

He notices an increasing booming type sound advancing towards him on the road.

A gaudy, election daubed, open-topped car is approaching, slowly.

The polished, political candidate is promoting his future policies.

Danny Trump is feeling particularly irritated.

Irritated, that this jumped up penguin is disturbing his already unpleasant journey to his personal purgatory.

"I will guarantee that the streets are safe to walk, that we will all have a minimum, guaranteed wage.

And I will personally guarantee that I am the future of this town, and …"

Danny strolls out directly in front of the vehicle, which is forced to stop, likewise, the politician.

The two undercover clowns face each other off.

"Please could you step out of my way?"

"Yeh, sure, just as soon as you guarantee to start telling the truth."

He doesn't really know why he has thought to say to say such a thing, but since all politicians are lairs, anyway, it just seemed a fun thing to respond.

"Please …"

"Tell the truth!"

For one microscopic instant, it seems that the whole world stops.

The small crowd waits…

"And I totally guarantee to do the least work possible, and to definitely guarantee to line my pockets as much as I can tax you for.

And to Tweet about how wonderful I am, on an hourly basis."

He smiles, and, feeling slightly better, heads off to work.

The bell rings; usually the voyagers would be ready in the aisle, and, once signalled, catapult themselves into the scrummage at the door, to reach the open space of the pavement.

Only, now, here, today, nobody dares to move.

Miss Thatcher stands immobile, perfectly presented, all the way from her impeccably combed hair, down to her spotlessly clean black shoes.

She had boarded the bus as usual, just outside the school gates at 3.45pm, after having patiently waited for the heaving mass of excited youth to catch the one before.

She was pleased to notice that there was a policeman sitting in one of the rows towards the front, some of the older teenagers could be rather boisterous.

True to her concerns, three stops later, two uncouth, youths got on and walked passed where she was sitting.

They plonked themselves down on one of the double seats further inside the bus.

She was already thinking to say something as they were resting their feet on the back on the seat in front.

It was then that one of them switched on their phone thingy and started playing some awful rap music.

Of course, the term 'music' would not be one that she would associate with that noise.

"Excuse me, but could you please turn that off."

"Y'what?"

"I asked, please would you be kind enough to stop that awful din."

"That's *$hitFace Doug*."

"I can totally relate to that, so please have mercy on the rest of us, and switch it off."

Then they did something totally unacceptable to her; they turned to each other, and then turned the volume higher.

Not being used to being ignored, and even less being disrespected, she stopped to look round for a solution.

"Officer, please can you do something to get those young hooligans to turn off their noise?"

"Sorry, ma'am but I'm now off duty and they don't seem to be disturbing anyone else but you."

She stopped for a moment, tension rising visibly through her body.

"Officer, do as you are told. Get up and stop that disgrace, that people now call music!"

The rest of the bus froze into silence as she screamed at the uniformed constable.

The bearded law-enforcer stopped for a moment before slowly turning 'round to look her, full in the face.

"Of course." And he immediately got up and walked over to the two music enthusiasts.

"You switch that off now or I will confiscate it."

"You can't do that, it's not allowed."

"Do you want to argue with me?" He was becoming menacing.

"Okay, it's no big deal," the music was stopped and the phone, pocketed.

He then mumbled something unpleasant under his breath, fortunately only his friend was close enough to hear.

Someone rang the bell for the bus to stop, but when it did, nobody moved.

Miss Thatcher stands immobile, perfectly presented, all the way from her impeccably combed hair, down to her spotlessly clean black shoes.

Ch 16. Somewhere, morning

Patricia awakens.

Her first reaction is to scream. "Noooooo," and throw herself across the room to escape the on-coming car.

Of course, there are no cars in the bizarre room in which she is now laying on the old, polished wooden floor.

"Ouch!"

"Yes, I suppose that throwing yourself onto the floor might be a little painful."

The little, green faced hunchback smiles down at her.

In pain from having thrown herself onto the floor, she now curls herself into a tight ball to protect herself from this mad mixture of the Wicked Witch of the West and a Munchkin.

Several seconds pass, and as nothing is happening, she slightly uncurls and asks, "what are you?"

"Are you okay?"

"No, I'm not!"

"Well, I suppose that throwing yourself across the room onto the floor is not really such a good idea," he repeats, as if expressing it for the first time.

She swears softly under her breath. Not knowing where she is, she decides not to antagonise him, unnecessarily.

"I thought that I was about to be hit by a car."

"Oh that, that was last night."

"What? But that was just now."

"Well, I suppose that one doesn't really notice time passing when one has turned oneself into a statue."

She turns around in shock to see the bent old crone who has just entered into the room.

"Oh my God, who are you?"

"Helen of Troy, pleased to meet you," the old hag curtsies elegantly.

The Bureau Of Regional & Internationally Negotiated Governmental policy.

The lights in the conference chamber are suitably dimmed to conserve energy, which makes it rather difficult to see the representatives at the far end of the chilly council chamber.

The Austrian delegate starts up in surprise. His thick, black glasses wobble, as he jerks his head up.

The table shakes as the elected chief executive pounds it energetically.

"This is not acceptable. We have spent years creating the perfect world. Everything is tidy, organised and ordered."

"But I'm sure that things are not so bad." The British deputy tries to reassure his fellow colleagues.

"No, it isn't, we no gotta' accept this." His thick, black moustache trembling with emotion.

He expresses as much with his heads as with his words, an Italian stereotype, if ever there was one.

In quiet German efficiency, the fat, balding Bavarian takes the floor.

"We have reports of a Swiss that can do weird things with time, and a French fräulein that turned her superior into a golden statue.

Then there is an English lady that can force people to do her every wish and an American guy that gets people to tell the total truth."

"Oh my God," someone murmurs from the far end of the table.

"And if that wasn't enough, someone in Alaska is messing about with the colour of our drinks."

"So, what would you suggest that we do?" The quite British delegate inquires.

A red light flashes, and all the computer terminals go blank.

Silence.

Then, simultaneously, they all see, printed in large, clear, red letters,

'THE BIG BOSS IS NOT HAPPY'…

Other Titles in the Less Boring Series

Slightly Less Boring

In this, the second book of the trilogy, we are introduced to even more less boring people, now that they also have super powers.

And we also continue to follow the lives of the 'heroes' that we have already met.

These people begin to be useful. According to the witch's plan.

But what of the B.O.R.I.N.G. world council?

The Boss who is 'Not Happy' Is creating a multi-phase plan to capture all the 'less borings'.

Not Boring

In this, the final chapter of the story, our super powered 'friends' are declared evil and dangerous by the B.O.R.I.N.G. world council.

How do they escape from their secure holding unit?

And what to do next?

A handful of untrained individuals against the heavily trained and armed forces of the council.

Who eventually, will win?

Or are they doomed to be recaptured and imprisoned for life?

Well, you'll just have to read it to find out.